Ad Infinitum

A Science Fiction Novella about
Time, Free Will, and Complexity

by
Randall R. Scott

For
Sarah, Brett, Robin
and my father

Randy Scott is retired and lives in St. Louis, Missouri. An academic pedestrian of no great importance for many years, his current interests include theoretical physics; literature; neuroscience; orchestral composition; religious and psychological studies; Japanese literary and emotional aesthetics (in translation); complexity and approximation; and, most especially, watching his granddaughter grow up in California.

Cover design by Randall R. Scott
Painting courtesy Zoë Sarafin Doyle

Ad Infinitum: A Science Fiction Novella about Time, Free Will, and Complexity
© 2020 Randall R. Scott
All rights reserved.

Contents

Chapter One

In Illud Tempus

IT WAS 6:26 P.M., OR THEREABOUTS. Ariana Laplace sat in her study at home and, almost against her will, stared at the old-fashioned analog clock on the wall, marked with its familiar, discrete units of time. Seconds, minutes, hours. Time. Linear time, flowing past the disconnected black concentric dashes on the clock's white face. She had been home for just a little while after a long day at the university, where she had given the semester's final exam – oral – for her only teaching assignment, a class of three graduate physics students. Pretty routine but still draining at forty-five minutes each. She slowly unwound with a cigarette and a glass of smooth, unblended scotch. Occasionally her mind would allow the many shelves of indecorously untidy books and papers to enter her peripheral field of view. But, for some reason, her eyes were fixed on the clock. The date was May 17, 2079.

Ariana Laplace was born in 2039 in Paris. Her father, Jean, was a research chemist and her mother, Sophie, was a clothing designer. She emigrated to America with them before she was a year old. She was now forty, and her lean and somewhat lined face spoke of both youth and age. Her black hair had begun to grey a bit here and there, and was now hanging long, past her shoulders. If you looked observantly at her dark features for any length of time, you saw not just an objective beauty but a subjective rarity – a *something* emanating from beneath her façade that spoke of complexity and a depth of mind and character. Somehow this inner something found its way to the surface. You could see it in her eyes. She was incessantly curious, and felt most alive when unexplored points of view suddenly presented themselves to her and irresistibly beckoned. Whether her love for original thinking precipitated her introversion or was a product of it, she didn't know, but in any case, her genius typically could not be reciprocated in conversation by more pedestrian thinkers, and that included most of her scientific colleagues.

Ariana was a resident professor of relativity and quantum dynamics at Princeton University's Institute for Advanced Study, one of the world's leading centers for academic research, particularly in mathematics and physics. Her job was mainly research, with minimal teaching responsibilities.[1] As a resident professor with a number of publications under her belt, Ariana had earned the right to *smell* – that is, to use her well-grounded instinct to controvert accepted theoretical postulates.

Ariana Laplace was primarily a relativist – a student of Einstein's theories of relativity, which after some one hundred fifty years were still in play. Since her doctoral and postdoc years she had been working, on and off, with Einstein's field equations regarding the block universe, particularly the unreality of time – or more precisely, the illusion of time's passage, time's arrow. The block universe theory stated that time was fundamentally unreal, its passage an illusion, with the future already somehow present and thus absolutely determined or locked in. Per Einstein, the universe *today* encompassed the entire past, present, and future. Einstein was convinced of this his entire life, despite the onset of quantum mechanics.[2] This static interpretation of time, the block universe, had never smelled right to her, despite the success of the relativistic mathematics.

As the clock stared back at her, Ariana absent-mindedly took off her glasses and squeezed the bridge of her nose. The phone rang.

"Answer, voice only," she said, releasing her nose and looking up. She hadn't activated caller ID, and didn't like surprise video calls.

She put on her glasses again, and a blank holographic screen materialized before her, from which a voice hurriedly said, "Alice, it's Bob."

That was her colleague's familiar, 'textbook' greeting. 'Bob' was her partner in professional physics crime, someone with whom she *could* engage in stimulating discussion. They were both perturbationists, as they sometimes called themselves, often feeling a palpable drive to counter the mainstream of physical theory with a minority report – if the parochial theory somehow didn't smell right, mathematics notwithstanding.

---

[1] Enrolling students – graduate-level only – at the Institute for Advanced Study was a recent expansion of the mission of the research facility, beginning with the fall semester of 2069. Only a very select number were accepted each year, and the student-professor ratio in the natural sciences was approximately 3 to 1.

[2] Einstein had stated bluntly in 1922 to an audience of philosophy academicians: "The time of the philosophers does not exist." In 1955, three weeks before his death, he persisted: "People like us, who believe in physics, know that the distinction between past, present, and future is only a stubbornly persistent illusion."

Bob's real name was Greyson Landon. Born in Boston to middle-class parents, he was thirty-four, six years younger than Ariana. His father, Paul, was of mixed Caribbean and European descent, and his mother, Grace, was also from a multi-ethnic background, most recently derived from New York's Lower East Side. Greyson was short in stature with a sturdy appearance and unkempt sandy blonde hair, and he had just been appointed resident professor at the Institute. But with only a few published articles to his name, he hadn't yet officially earned the right to smell. His nose nevertheless was quite functional. That's what drew Ariana (and Princeton) to seek his company – not only his intellect, but his instincts, which rivaled her own. Greyson Landon's area was quantum mechanics. Together, Ariana and Greyson made a good team.

"On screen," she said to the hologram. Greyson appeared on-screen from the waist up in a navy blue t-shirt, sitting behind a desk in a nondescript office, leaning forward. His face was ashen, his hair more untended than usual, and he was a bit out of breath. He looked like he'd been up for days. The noise of people shouting and conversing over each other was in the background.

"Ariana…. Ariana, there's…there's been an accident," he said, without continuing a more cordial greeting.

"Grey, what are you talking about?"

"At the new facility…at the lepton collider. I'm here now. I don't know what's going to happen – hell, I don't even know what's happening *now!*" There was a break in his voice and alarm in his eyes.

* * * * * * * * * * * *

The 'lepton collider' was the Institute's pet name for the recently completed Lepton Degeneracy Stabilizer – usually called the LDS for short. The theoretical groundwork had been done at the Institute, and Ariana had been on the research team. The technology had been forged and built at the Massachusetts Institute of Technology (MIT) in Cambridge, in concert primarily with Princeton's Institute, but also in association with hundreds of other physicists and engineers from around the world.

The LDS was not yet online at MIT but was partially operational, still in the testing phase. It's mission was to probe whether a proposed *temporal* corollary of the Pauli exclusion principle was possible.[3] Electrons and their antiparticles, positrons, when forced physically together into a very dense co-locating state, might create a unique variant of what in physics was known as degeneracy pressure.[4] Predictive calculations and quantum supercomputer modeling had shown that this co-location might create what had been termed *bitemporal* degeneracy pressure. Since electrons obey the normal, future-facing arrow of time, and positrons travel backward in time, into the past,[5] co-locating them might yield very interesting *temporal* results. The nature of time had always been an issue in physics, and natural philosophy before it, and this experiment might reveal some new information. There was no mathematical consensus on what, exactly, that information might be. There were mathematical predictions, and quantum supercomputer modeling, but no agreement, including on the meaning of the word 'bitemporal.'

The physical co-location of electrons and positrons would be accomplished by a new technology never before deployed outside a phase-two prototype in the MIT lab. The technology was called quantum gravity generation, and the unit was called the QG2 – for Quantum Gravity Generator.[6] The QG2 was designed to compress or warp spacetime – to manufacture an incredibly strong gravitational field – but only on very small and delimited scale, assuring the safety of the adjacent environment. In

---

[3] The Pauli exclusion principle is the quantum mechanical law that states that two or more identical fermions cannot simultaneously occupy the same quantum state within a quantum system. The law is, for instance, what keeps electrons from collapsing into the nucleus of atoms.

[4] Normally, combining matter and antimatter results in mutual annihilation, but theoretically – that is, per the project calculations and under the controlled conditions of the experiment – it was now thought that the annihilation of the electrons and positrons would be averted. (After all, the meson – that 'peaceful' but very short-lived combination of a quark and an antiquark – had been part of the Standard Model since the mid-twentieth century.) Just what would result from the electron-positron co-location was a major purpose of the LDS experiment.

[5] Richard Feynman had published initial research in this general area over a century earlier (cf. Phys. Rev. 76, 749 – 15 September 1949), followed most notably by the "Goldberg Lectures" of Samaka Ellsworth Goldberg at MIT in 2035.

[6] The problem of 'quantum gravity,' as it came to be called around the turn of the twenty-first century, had not been solved. 'Quantum gravity generation' was merely the phrase used to describe the method of radically warping spacetime on a very small (but not quantum) and quite delimited (and thus safe) scale. Quantum mechanics were involved, thus the name. (Think of it as a sort of warp drive for leptons.)

theory, the QG2 had the capability of creating a small but contained gravitational field as strong as that of a neutron star.

The 'stabilizer' part the Lepton Degeneracy Stabilizer, the technology for which had been only recently been developed specifically for this project, was required to prevent gravity from exceeding specified limits so that the co-located particles would be in no danger of collapsing into a microscopic black hole.

Physicists hoped the collider would, after millennia of philosophical palaver, be capable of no less than empirically revealing a *physical* nature to time itself.

* * * * * * * * * * * *

Greyson was onsite at the LDS facility at MIT because he was helping to oversee the machine's final calibrations and test runs. Ariana had been aware of his involvement in the project – which was partly based, in fact, on her Ph.D. research some years earlier – but Greyson's urgent phone call was completely unexpected.

"What do you *mean* you don't know what's happening now?" Ariana said. She began to tense up. "What *is* happening now?"

"We need you to come to Cambridge immediately," replied Greyson, nearly interrupting. It was obvious there wasn't time to explain. "Get in your bladerunner and get here now! We need you!" The screen went blank. Greyson had either hung up or was disconnected.

Ariana, feeling a rising tension, quickly gathered her things, went outside and got into her bladerunner. Bladerunners were what people called their thruster-driven self-flying cars, recalling the two iconic films of the late twentieth and early twenty-first centuries.[7] The bladerunner would be much faster than the high-speed train, and she could land just outside the LDS facility at MIT. Before the car door had finished closing, she had punched-in her destination and touched the start button. The car's thrusters slowly lifted it to several hundred feet and then accelerated it up and forward toward a free-and-clear navigation altitude, typically around 8,000 feet. Everything

---

[7] Piloted flying cars, or bladerunners, had been commercially available to the general public since 2042, but only recently had become mainstream thanks to a new constellation of sixty-four GPS satellites, dedicated solely to their safe, automated navigation.

was automated. The trip to Cambridge was around two hundred fifty miles and would take thirty-seven minutes.

When the bladerunner of Ariana Laplace landed itself in the front parking lot of the LDS facility in Cambridge, it was 7:49 p.m. Night had just fallen, and the grounds were buzzing with people and activity. Greyson Landon was outside waiting.

Chapter Two

The Accident in the Lab

AS THE BLADERUNNER DOOR SLOWLY SWUNG UPWARD to let Ariana out, she could see dozens of people running in and out of the LDS entrances and exits, and dozens of others were crowded and milling in separate enclaves away from the eight-story building. Lights from large emergency vehicles, both road trucks on the ground and aerial bladerunner trucks at station-keeping above, were already turning night into day around the facility. As she was getting out, an agitated Greyson, speaking over the background noise, was already in the middle of his second or third truncated sentence: "...a power surge during a safety test. Don't know why. Our calibrations weren't finalized. But the system *came online*. I think. Don't know for sure. The premix injectors and magnets are hot, and it looks like a large number of electrons and positrons escaped into the co-location core – *before the stabilizer was ready*.... We weren't *ready*, Ariana!"

The lepton co-location core was on the lowest level of the LDS facility, twelve hundred feet below ground. The entire physical plant at that level, the real workings of the LDS, occupied a room almost the size of a football field, with a ceiling of over one hundred feet.

Greyson, obviously quite upset, rambled on, "Down there, at the level of the collider, the core.... When the surge came. People began to feel dizzy. Faint. *Disoriented*. They're being checked out now at the university clinic. They seem alright from what I hear. We evacuated everyone but essential personnel. A few quantum and mechanical engineers are still down there. They tell me most of the equipment function now seems nominal. But I don't know. We don't *think* there's any indication of an imminent explosion, or implosion, or.... But...."

He stopped, trying not to breathe too heavily, and looked at her in an odd way, with both questions and answers in his eyes. Ariana had always been very observant, and had seen him look that way before.

13

Mysterium tremendum, mysterium fascinosum, she thought to herself.[8] Her eyes darted unfocused to the distance and her mind quickly scanned the possibilities of what the imminent future might have in store. Then her attention swung back to her friend, and she grasped Greyson's shoulder and leaned in.

"But what, Grey?" she said, looking him in the eye and speaking in a tone that was barely audible above the noise of people and machines.

"Ti…," Greyson began to say.

"Professor Landon!" At that moment Ariana and Greyson were interrupted by a woman running up to them in an open white lab coat, holding a yellow safety helmet on her head as she ran. It was Eloise Bardier, a senior quantum engineer on the project, with whose team Greyson had been working closely on the final stabilizer calibrations. She was out of breath and in what looked like a condition of controlled distress.

Eloise shouted over the confusion, "Greyson — we've achieved shutdown of all LDS systems, except that *the core is not responding.* It's still…. There's still…. There's still *something* going on in the core. The gravitational field is *increasing.* Co-location has…. And without the stabilizer…. You and Professor Laplace had better come. *Now.*"

Ariana, Greyson, and Eloise all ran into the LDS building and entered turbolift for the trip down. It was 8:20 p.m., less than two hours after Greyson had first called Ariana. Eloise quickly pressed the bottom button, marked "Plant" for the LDS machinery, the lowest level, and the turbolift emitted a low-frequency hum as it transitioned slowly into its rapid descent to twelve hundred feet underground.

Less than two minutes later, the turbolift doors opened onto the large LDS expanse. It was 8:22 p.m. The only illumination was from the emergency back-up lights, and except for a few key personnel who were

---

[8] Although fully dedicated to the scientific method, Ariana had spent considerable time in her youth exploring literary masterworks of fiction and reading the classics of religious studies, including *The Idea of the Holy* by Rudolf Otto. She also continued to dabble in cognitive neuroscience since the flow of time and the neurological mechanisms for memory seemed obviously related. She had always considered that reading the great minds in other disciplines was as central to her identity as her more recent, primary work in theoretical physics. Were some of these disciplines, such as science and religion, non-overlapping magisteria? Of course. And yet being conversant in multiple disciplines added complexity to her thought.

obviously in very serious consultation with each other, there was an eerie silence in the cavernous air. One of the engineers quickly walked over to them.

"Eloise," said Juan Marcelino, a senior mechanical engineer, with a slight Chilean accent. The emergency lights were shining on his dark complexion that was bearing a two-day growth of beard. "Eloise, everything's shut down," said Juan, "or is in the process of shutting down, but the core is still exhibiting...it's exhibiting fluctuations. Dynamic fluctuations."

"What do you mean, dynamic fluctuations?" said Eloise.

Juan didn't speak, but looked at Greyson. Greyson indicated with a nod that he should continue.

"Radiation," Juan said. "But not the usual kind."

Ariana broke in, "Not the usual kind?"

"It appears that within the core, the QG2 gravity engaged. The core was already flooded with electrons and positrons, but without the stabilizer in place.... Juan paused. "The gravity...."

"Don't tell me you've created a *microscopic black hole*?" Ariana exclaimed. She unconsciously took a half-step backward.

Juan shook his head but had trouble getting the next sentence out of his mouth.

Greyson continued for him: "Not a microscopic black hole, Ariana. Not *yet*, anyway. The radiation is.... It seems to be *temporal* radiation. It's *time*, Ariana – *time*. Not spacetime. Not space. Time. *Time* is in flux, or appears to be, or *something*, in the core. The monitors in the core room have gone dark. But the anomaly seemed to be *radiating*, maybe getting larger, expanding. I don't know exactly how to describe it, but it seems the electrons and positrons *have* been co-located. We won't know for sure until we get back in there." Ariana noticed the worry in his eyes.

Greyson continued: "I guess you could call the accident...a success. Of sorts. But there's danger. Or potential danger. *Who knows?* Inside the core, Ariana, time is not...*behaving*. That's why we called you. We need a relativist, and we need *you* in particular, Ariana. The best. Someone who's been looking at this for years."

And then he continued by unconsciously summing up: "It's not a spacetime black hole, Professor Laplace," applying some formality to his words. "It appears we've created *temporal* black hole. A *hole in time*,

Ariana…. Or a bubble. Or a hole in space. We don't know what to call it, and we really don't know what this means -- or how to deal with it."

"A hole in *time*? A bubble *of* time?" Ariana repeated back to him. "That's not possible. I mean, I've actually attempted the calculations a number of times. I mean, I've done the bookkeeping. Even in my doctoral work. I tried to isolate time from space in my thesis, and the math, the logic…just doesn't seem to work. *Infinities* crop up. I did come up with some creative hypotheses, but I really don't think it's possible."

A second went by. "Maybe not," Greyson responded, now strangely calm, with a very slight upturn of a smile, his eyes getting a bit wider as he looked at her, disregarding for a moment the threat of any immediate catastrophe. Ariana suddenly became aware. Their minds were on the same page.

And then the noise began.

* * * * * * * * * * * *

Greyson was familiar with Ariana's work, of course: The block universe of Einstein and its place in mainstream physics. The arrow of time. Is it an illusion? Is the future statically determined (*pre*determined was out of the question because in Einstein's theory there was no '*pre*') based on Einstein's own interpretation of his equations? Is the universe tenseless? Does the future already exist, only to be *happened upon* at a moment that isn't *now*?

Or – is time real? Are time and its arrow – or arrows, forward and reverse – *actually real*? Fundamental? Is time's flow something that unfolded based largely on the present moment, the continuous *now*, not just billions of years ago at the original moment of inflation and the Big Bang? Is there a *currency* to time? Is an open future *permissible* per undiscovered or reinterpreted physical laws? And if so, does the human mind, human consciousness, the human *will* have a bearing on the inextricable events by which time is measured? If change *does* in fact exist, do we have *agency* with regard to that change? Can we participate in the change?

To the latter questions, the block universe theory, as calculated by Einstein, emphatically said no.[9]

* * * * * * * * * * * * *

"Gödel," Ariana said, as the noise began, in the echo of Grey's quixotic words "Maybe not."[10] Whatever was happening in the core room, perhaps discovery was at hand, perhaps something beyond the mathematics. And then she thought the thought that had comforted her many, many times: *To gain in complexity is to gain on reality.* This thought had become the most important of her credos, and so she repeated it in her mind:

To gain in complexity is to gain on reality.

Whatever was happening, they were probably about to enter new territory. Turning her back on the group in front of the turbolift, she walked some seventy-five feet to the core room, the noise level increasing with every step. The sound of alarms joined the unfamiliar noise. Seemingly oblivious to the obvious threat of danger, she pushed opened the heavy metal door and walked in.

---

[9] There was also the question of neuroscience – the mind-brain complex. In this particular case, the relation of time's arrow and the brain comprised part of what was known as "the binding problem." Was time only a manufactured product of the mind-brain complex – an organic phenomenon based on chemoelectrical neural encoding of events and a forward-facing interpretation of such code – that is, memory and anticipation? Was time only a convenient measuring rod of consciousness? Was time all in one's head? This wasn't her field, but it was obviously involved, and Ariana felt the need to stay abreast.

[10] Kurt Gödel, the famous Austrian mathematical logician had shown – *proved* – in 1930 (published 1931) that mathematical reality, in an ideal or ultimate sense, *must* transcend any formal attempt to express or articulate it. In his "incompleteness theorems," Gödel had *proved* the true but unprovable. One cannot fully examine or articulate a formal system from *within* that system. Such examination is, in the final analysis, incomplete. Gödel had thereby suggested that perhaps there is a reality beyond our symbols to express it. Ariana had given this much thought, and discussed the subject with Greyson. Kurt Gödel had taken up permanent resident appointment, after all, at the Institute for Advanced Study in 1940. Einstein and Gödel were close friends there during the mid-twentieth century, often taking long walks together to discuss their work, so Ariana had examined Gödel's work closely. If Einstein could walk with Gödel, so should she.

Chapter Three
A Superposition of Time

IT WAS APPROACHING 8:59 P.M. WHEN Ariana entered the core room with Greyson, Eloise, and Juan in close pursuit. They started to follow her in but Ariana gestured to them to remain outside due to the alarms. They reluctantly complied, and looked into the core room of the LDS plant through the large, reinforced plate-glass window. Inside was Ariana, scanning everything with her eyes and her mind, trying to determine what was happening. It was just after 8:59 p.m. per their respective caesium-powered watches, which were in agreement. The quantum clock, the quark-powered clock on the inside wall of the chamber, was digitally displaying the same time, though to four decimal places following the seconds digit.

The quark-powered clock was the first thing Ariana noticed when she entered the core room. The clock was on the wall immediately behind the core's outer sphere, which was ten meters in diameter and covered in thick, multilayered gold foil to aid in thermal containment. Her eyes fixated on the golden sphere. Inside the golden outer sphere of the core, out of view, two independent particle receptor chambers, hemispheric in shape, had been constructed, one for electrons and the other for positrons. Each particle chamber was fed by seven large intake conduits that were sourced by a number of premix injectors.

The quantum gravity generator itself – the QG2 – consisted of two circular 'halo orbitals' of niobium tin superconducting magnets, one orbital slightly contained within the other, encircling the outer sphere. The magnetic orbitals were what generated the strong gravitation field deep inside the sphere, and they also assisted the stabilizer in the containment of the gravity. The orbitals of the QG2 were currently circumambulating each other at orthogonal angles in what appeared to be nearly perpetual motion, but were in the process of slowly coming to a halt due to the shutdown.

The stabilizer power unit, a large and mostly standalone machine in its own right, was connected to the magnets and the outer sphere by a vast array of electrical and optical cables, laser transmitters, energy-displacement actuators, and a series of differential valves.

Inside the ten-meter sphere and beyond the particle chambers, at the very heart of the core, was the Inner Gravitational Chamber, the IGC – the actual target area of the QG2 field and the electron and positron co-location. The IGC sphere measured a mere ten centimeters in diameter.

On the wall behind the outer gold-covered sphere, under the clock, there were six large physical computer screens that monitored the entire LDS system. Though they had shut down at the initial power surge, they were now displaying minimal information, and the numerous red and orange warning lights were sounding their respective emergency alarms, despite the system shutdown. Alarms aside, the noise level in the room was rising steadily, dominated by something that now sounded like an overload.

As Ariana stepped toward the monitors and studied them, it quickly became apparent to her that co-location *was occurring* – with a stabilizer that, at last measurement before shutdown, was *far* from being calibrated within specifications. That meant that the degeneracy pressure limit – to prevent any collapse of spacetime inside the IGC into a microscopic black hole – would not hold. And yet a black hole had not formed and did not appear to be forming. Not in the usual sense, anyway. Not per the limited information on monitors at any rate, she judged. The IGC had been flooded with time-forward electrons and time-reverse positrons, and the warping of spacetime there was oscillating dynamically, randomly it seemed – first stronger, then weaker, then weaker still, then more strongly again. The gravimetric reading of the IGC monitors didn't make sense. It seemed like a chain reaction of some kind was in progress.

"What in the *hell* is going on?" she said, analyzing aloud to herself, surprised at her lack of panic. "Without the stabilizer in place, the gravitational field should intensify, perhaps indefinitely. So why is it fluctuating? Why aren't we seeing a black hole? I just don't understand those readings." Her innate curiosity prevented the sense of relief that she should have felt from not seeing a black hole in formation. She then motioned toward the plate-glass window for Grey, Eloise, and Juan to join her inside.

She wasn't indicating safety as much as a bizarre scientific anomaly that she thought they would want to directly experience for themselves.

As the three others quickly entered the core room to join her, she looked again at the clock on the wall, expecting it to read 9:03 p.m. or so — only now she couldn't read it. Not precisely. The digital clock face appeared to bend or wave slowly, first in focus and then blurred. And what was more, the numbers *seemed* to be racing this way and that, higher then lower, forward and then back, and then forward again. But that couldn't be. It was like the clock was being hit by a temporal interference pattern.

"What the...?" she muttered. Then she remembered Grey's words. *A temporal black hole. A hole in time.* A bubble *of* time. All of a sudden she began to feel somewhat disoriented — as though her own consciousness was being hit by a temporal interference pattern.

Eloise Bardier shouted over the noise: "Are you all seeing this? The clock.... The metrics on the monitors...." As she spoke, she noticed that everywhere she looked, things were beginning to look...*strange*. There seemed to be a translucent, undulating field of some kind materializing in the room before her, outward from the core. Or perhaps the entire room itself was undulating.

Greyson nodded in agreement, then he also began to feel a bit dizzy. "It's just like a little while ago, only stronger," he said loudly over the rising background noise. "Now *I* feel it, or I feel...*something*. The radiation still seems to be growing. I don't understand how, but I *think* space is being *separated* from time, *somehow*. Displaced. Stripped away. Must be due to the collision of time's arrows...the co-location of the electrons and positrons."

Juan shouted, "Do you... Do you think that...." He could barely hear himself over the noise.

Greyson interrupted loudly: "I think we may have just witnessed decohered quantum particles revert back into a cohered superposition." He was having to practically scream to be heard over the still-increasing ambient whine. And then he thought to himself: *A temporal superposition. A growing temporal superposition of classical proportions.* This *was* unknown territory.

Just then the deafening overload whine started changing. The plaintive high-pitched groan was becoming more of a steady pulsing sound, as though a crest had been reached and was receding into something less dangerous, but also less...familiar. The red and orange warning lights on the monitors went dark and their respective audible alarms abruptly stopped.

Juan was now able to make himself heard in the still-pulsating room: "It's as though the co-location of the particles is creating a reality of *purified time*. First in the core, and now out here. Time that has no space. A hole.... A temporal hole that leads.... I don't know where, or...." He stopped, having lost his train of thought.

Eloise finished his thought for him, "Or *when*." Then looking around the core room, Eloise noticed that the pulsing sound seemed to be synchronizing with the visible undulating phenomenon that filled in the room, and she began to feel faint as the anomaly swept through her. She'd never felt like this before, so it was impossible to quickly describe the experience to herself – intellectually, emotionally. She wondered if she was disappearing to some degree, in some way, or if perhaps the *room around her* was disappearing – not completely, though. Only up to a point. She was still there. The room was still there. But she still felt a part of something strange, something deep, something fundamental, below which there was nothing, there *could be* nothing. That's what it *felt* like, anyway. She grabbed a nearby steel support-beam to steady herself. She tried to focus, but her consciousness and her surroundings melted into each other.

Chapter Four

To Gain in Complexity

IT WAS 2063, SOME SIXTEEN YEARS BEFORE THE INCIDENT at the LDS. Ariana Laplace, age twenty-four, was working as a doctoral student in relativistic quantum dynamics at the California Institute of Technology – Caltech – in Pasadena. Caltech had been home to the likes of Richard Feynman, Murray Gell-Man, Kip Thorne, and Victoria Beckerman, and was now, in 2063, the home of her dissertation advisor, Hans Porter – all of whom had been recipients of 'the Swedish prize,' as physicists called it: the Nobel Prize in Physics.[11]

Her thesis, in progress under Hans Porter, a mathematical physicist, was in the general area of trying to reinterpret, if possible, Einstein's field equations in light of the lingering questions concerning the sacrosanct tradition of the deterministic block universe.

The block universe and its attendant determinism had to do with a fundamental scientific understanding of causality, or the lack thereof; free will, or the lack thereof; and the flow of time (past, present, and future), or the lack thereof.

New interpretations of quantum theory, along with advances in cognitive neuroscience, quantum biochemistry, and complexity science in general, had finally accumulated to the point of a critical mass, casting an even longer shadow of doubt on the absolutely deterministic view of reality required by relativity. In short, it looked as though Einstein needed a rewrite. An interrelational *science of complexity* had emerged, a

---

[11] Richard Feynman, 1965, for his work in quantum electrodynamics (QED). Murray Gell-Mann, 1969, for his work in elementary particles. Kip Thorne, 2017, for his contribution in building the first generation of LIGO detectors and the consequent observation of gravitational waves. Victoria Beckerman, 2032, for her work in the dynamic structure of quantum fields. Hans Porter, 2055, for his work in mathematically formalizing the turbulent electromagnetic patterns that had been recently detected in the Cosmic Microwave Background (CMB) radiation, c. 380,000 years after the birth of the universe. These turbulent patterns in the polarization of the CMB were thought to have been caused, in large part, by the gravitational waves at the very birth of the universe.

new paradigm, in which *everything was seen as influencing everything else.* Nonlinear science. As a result, the traditional method of doing 'physics in a box' — whether blithely isolating systems from the rest of the universe for the purpose of convenient measurement, or ignoring important findings of your natural science colleagues across the quadrangle – now entailed significant professional peril.

The other deterministic doctrine, known as 'Laplace's demon' (no relation to Ariana) – that early nineteenth-century omniscient, deterministic, cause-and-effect anathema to free will[12] – had died, of course, with the discovery of the random and uncertain realities inherent in the quantum world. Niels Bohr, Werner Heisenberg, and Erwin Schrödinger, among others, had seen to that in the early twentieth century. But the ghost of Laplace's deterministic demon had continued to wander the halls of science for over a century thereafter, despite the indisputable stochastic nature of quantum mechanics, from which the classical or macroscopic world was known to emerge. Despite the demise of Laplace's demon, the block universe theory of relativity, also purely deterministic, lingered.

In contradistinction to determinism, complexity collaborations in the fields of cognitive neuroscience and quantum biochemistry had shown that even at the molecular level, reality emerges not just from a bottom-up obedience to physical law, but from a *top-down leverage* applied by a conscious mind. It had been empirically demonstrated that the human mind *does* chemoelectrically affect the physical brain from which it somehow emerged long ago. The interdependent complexities of physics, biochemistry, and neuroscience had proven that mental states *do* change physical states – that reality *is*, in fact, to some extent, in one's head, or at least can start there.[13]

---

[12] The thought experiment of Pierre-Simon Laplace (1749-1827) of course had involved an omniscient intelligence which, knowing all the initial conditions of the universe and knowing all physical laws, could with absolute accuracy determine the fate of every particle, atom, molecule, and amalgam of molecules – such as human beings and the societies they comprise – until the end of time. By analogy, until fairly recently it had been thought that, given infinite data and infinite quantum computing power, one could theoretically concoct a mathematical proof for determinism.

[13] Cf. the late twentieth century works of Michael S. Gazzaniga, the father of cognitive neuroscience, and the quantum biochemistry works of Gabriel Borges during the mid-twenty-first century. Also, Ariana was well aware that the differentiation between "mental" and "physical" states was in fact to some degree an artifice of metaphor, since the

For most scientists today, in 2063, entertaining the notion that all the languages, all the thoughts, all the emotions, all the knowledge, all the imaginings, all the books, all the inventions, all the art and music, and all the science of all the conscious beings on all the (surely) inhabited planets in all the universe had been solely based on and determined by the initial conditions at inflation and the Big Bang seemed as preposterous as stating categorically that the moon was made of green cheese.

Yet the block universe theory lingered. For some reason, the deterministic block universe of Einstein was still – very oddly – an anachronistic thorn in the side of physics. A throwback. An almost inexplicable holdout. Like the ghost of Laplace's deterministic demon, the block universe also continued to show up in textbooks, but not in the obituary column. With few exceptions, the problematic block universe quite frankly had been unaddressed, unchallenged, and even ignored for a very long time.[14] But surely it must be as wrong as the notion of Laplace's demon, Ariana had always thought.

While *absolute* reality was known to still always be out of reach – infinity by definition being ungraspable by the human mind – the new interrelational complexity paradigm had matured to the point that Ariana had authored the credo that became, in fact, the bedrock and groundswell of all her professional endeavor: *To gain in complexity is to gain on reality.* And the goal of the scientist, her goal, was to gain on reality, even if that meant displacing the theories of giants. If Einstein's macrocosmic theories of relativity were incomplete, even considering the classical scale only, or were more approximate than historically thought, or if Einstein's laws were actually in error, at least regarding the illusory nature of time's

---

cerebral theater of activity was a unified physical mind/brain complex. Still, the metaphor had significant validity since it was universally agreed that consciousness was an emergent phenomenon. One chemoelectrical neuron does not consciousness make, just as one molecule of water is not wet, and one photon has no temperature (only energy). The quality of being wet and hot were emergent phenomena, too.

[14] Exceptions to this aversion included the proposals of the Perimeter Institute physicist Lee Smolin and Brazilian philosopher Roberto Mangabeira Unger during the early twenty-first century. Cf. *The Singular Universe and the Reality of Time* (Unger and Smolin, Oxford University Press, 2015) and *Time Reborn* (Smolin, First Mariner Books, 2014). New interpretation was also presented in the more recent work, *The Evolution of Time* by Anna K. Robinson and Roberto Salazar Bandes (Chronos Publications, 2047).

flow, she had to make definitive progress in her dissertation on how and why.[15]

* * * * * * * * * * * * *

Hans Porter, Ariana's thesis advisor, happened by Ariana's doctoral office at Caltech on a Friday afternoon in March 2063 while she was staring at her holographic computer screen and deep in thought.   He paused in the doorway.[16]

"How's the work coming?" he asked.

Hans Porter was born in Manchester, England, and educated at Churchill College, Cambridge University, and was now seventy.   His features were heavily lined but lively, and he sported a receding white hairline combed neatly back and a smile that never seemed far away.   He gave the impression that a lifetime of research and teaching, mostly at Caltech, had been as much a gift as a grind.   His Manchester accent had faded but was still slightly recognizable.

"Good question," she responded, looking up and wryly smiling. Hans smiled back.   He wasn't monitoring her progress.   There was no need for that.   Rather, he was sincerely and keenly interested in her work, knowing that her synapses fired just as quickly as his.

---

[15] It was well known that Einstein himself, though thoroughly convinced of his objective view on reality and on the illusory nature of past, present, and future, confided in correspondence with friends that he was still puzzled by the palpable, universal awareness of the subjective moment – on what 'now' meant in the face of his own theory.

Kurt Gödel, in honor of Einstein's seventh birthday, presented him with his own interpretation of the field equations, pronouncing that 'closed time loops' were the answer – that 'now' moments repeat themselves periodically.   Time's flow per Gödel was more like a real whirlpool than an illusory arrow.   Einstein, upon reviewing the calculations of his great friend, admitted that Gödel's interpretation of his field equations was possible, but mused, no doubt with a twinkle in his eye, that it should probably be dismissed on the basis of 'physical grounds.'

[16] Most doctoral students had offices tucked away here and there on campus, but Ariana's office was in brand new Richard P. Feynman Center for Theoretical Physics, on the same floor as the offices of many senior faculty members, including Hans Porter.   Ariana's star was rising.   (Caltech, and Hans Porter in particular, had begun to earnestly seek her professional company after she had done a summer internship in Pasadena while she was an undergraduate at Berkeley.)

"I think I've begun to see some new directions," she said. "When I insert the math into the complexity paradigm – into a real, evolving time scenario – new thoughts hit me. I'm pretty excited."

"Coming from you, promising indeed," said Hans over his dark, circular, professorial glasses.

Since her field was relativistic quantum dynamics, she was learning to be conversant in both the classical and quantum worlds, and the title of her dissertation reflected this inclusive fluency: *Chronometric Properties of Leptons Under Strong Gravitational Fields.* The title was typically dry and the focus by doctoral necessity was extremely specific, but Ariana hoped its underlying assumptions would be at least somewhat revolutionary. It was to be a combination of theory *and* hypothesis, something Ph.D. students were usually not allowed to do. For instance, some of the requisite technology for testing what she was proposing was still on the drawing board, but it was feasible given the funding.

She knew, in other words, that she was reaching, on the edge of things, pushing the boundary, but Professor Porter, the Nobel laureate, had given Ariana a free hand in exploring any possibilities – as long as her ideas were based in calculation and were empirically falsifiable in principle.[17] She was that smart. She was that promising. Hans Porter *wanted* something edgy from her, something that straddled the line of demarcation between science and philosophy, recalling the golden days of John Archibald Wheeler and *his* doctoral student, Richard P. Feynman, during the mid-twentieth century. They had *fun!* Those golden days of theoretical physics should and could come again, he had always thought.

Ariana replied formally to his compliment: "Thank you, professor. I think things are becoming more clear to me, at least from a distance. I find it hard to believe this train of thought has not already been thoroughly investigated before."

Hans Porter, the Nobel winner, looked at her silently, waiting for her to continue.

---

[17] The "Falsifiable Principle" mandate of science had been put forth by the twentieth-century philosopher of science, Karl Popper (1902-1994), to establish what was known as the line of 'demarcation' between actual science, on the one hand, and philosophy, on the other. The line was generally drawn with falsifiability in mind – that is, with the capacity to be proven wrong. Scientific theories, statements, and hypotheses must at least be falsifiable 'in principle' per Popper – if current technology did not yet admit experimental testing by way of observation/measurement.

"Relativity," she said. "With regard to the nature of time and its flow. Einstein's notion of a past, present, and future as a 'stubbornly persistent illusion' has survived, well, *stubbornly and persistently*, despite the empirical findings to the contrary by other scientific disciplines and of course quantum mechanics, too.[18]

"Take neuroscience. Take quantum biochemistry." She paused, thinking, then continued, "And *my* guess is that the social sciences have also played a role in the persistent notion in physics that time is not real. Social sciences *focus* on flow, change, evolution – all time-related. Consider them nearly self-evident, even. I think our physical colleagues are reluctant to be lumped into the same camp as those 'soft' sciences. Hierarchy, egos, and so forth," she concluded.

The kernel of her doctoral exploration, in the math and in the logic, was that time and its flow are *real*. Change happens. *Really*. The universe and everything in it has evolved. *Everything* has changed, is changing, and will continue to change, in complex, often nonlinear, and interrelated ways – *over time*. Everything will continue to affect everything else, in both predictable *and surprising* ways. (She didn't use the term *self-evident* easily, but in this case, from the complexity point of view, self-evident certainly seemed to apply. She of course could not use that term in her dissertation. She had to make her case, and conclusively so.) That was the "chronometric" part of her argument. Taking time and its measurement of change *seriously*.

Hans Porter, the mathematical physicist, knew her mind and was listening very intently, without pressing her for details just yet.

"The trick will be," she said, "to adjust the mathematics to include, as much as possible, the dynamical evolution of a complex world. Or at the very least, to show how our interpretation of mathematics will need to evolve as well into something a bit more...humble."

He knew what she was talking about, of course. He was, after all, a Nobel prize-winning mathematical physicist. Mathematics had always been done on small, isolated, constituent systems that were then presumed to scale-up accurately to the universe as a whole. And mathematics had always stamped a timeless fixity onto systems that quite obviously *were evolving in time*. This evolution over time of all that exists was self-

---

[18] See note 2 above.

evident in his opinion, too. Existence, reality, *being* itself were first and foremost about *becoming*. It was time for the mathematics to acknowledge that.

Ariana had to be especially careful not only in the mathematics but in the language of her dissertation. Language, like math, in the face of complexity was a blunt instrument, she knew. Her dissertation, while hopefully groundbreaking, would also be, in another sense, as transient as everything else in the universe and as inadequate a descriptor. Still, careful and clear articulation would, of course, go far toward making her argument.

"Well, I'll leave you to it," said Hans Porter, withdrawing from the doorway, turning, and beginning the walk down the hall to his office. It was around 5:00 p.m. Almost immediately another face sheepishly appeared at her office door.

"Professor Laplace?" a voice said. The noise of thruster-driven bladerunners taking off outside her office window at the end of the workweek almost made his tentative voice inaudible. She looked up and saw a young man of eighteen with a sturdy appearance and unkempt sandy blonde hair. He was one of her freshman students for the spring term. She recognized him because she was aware the young man was on full academic scholarship at Caltech. Professors tended to notice those things.

"Greyson Landon," she said.

Chapter Five

A Live One

"WHAT BRINGS YOU BY THE OFFICE at the end of a week?" she said cordially, looking over in his direction from the holographic computer screen hovering midair directly in front of her. She had seen Greyson Landon's university entrance test scores, and during her Relativity 224 lectures that term in Victoria Beckerman Hall[19] she could spot the wheels turning in his head as she spoke. *That* was a rare treat, even among scholarship students. His was the brightest face in the class of some two hundred students, and he always sat in the same seat in the first row.

"I heard you mention what you were working on in your dissertation, Professor," said Greyson, obviously not shy about popping in to ask questions of his professors. "About Einstein's view on the unreality of time. The unreality of the arrow of time, more precisely. Time as a static thing, deep down. I've been very curious about that myself." He spoke with a slight Bostonian accent.

Turning her chair toward him and nodding toward the extra chair in her office, she said kindly, "Please, Greyson, have a seat. What are your thoughts?" She saved her computer file and turned off the holoscreen, which promptly disappeared from in front of her.

"You know, what do *I* know?" said Greyson, sitting down. "I'm only a freshman. I just got here, last fall I mean. A public school kid from Boston. But I've spent most of my teenage years reading physics and watching science video lectures on the various platforms, and believe it or not, I've had some of the same questions. If the flow of time isn't real, really real, where does that leave the notion of causality? Does causality not really exist? And what about agency: Is *agency* an illusion, too — agency being really the same thing as causality. Are we merely along for the ride? Do we just *pretend* that causality and agency exist?

---

[19] See note 11 above.

"Go on," she said, feigning only casual interest, and not at all put off by the somewhat ambiguous, convoluted weave of his thoughts.

"I mean, are the mathematics and the physics of causality just expressions of a *pretense*? It seems like physics wants to have it both ways – time and its arrow being real with respect to causality, and being unreal when we step back and look at the so-called 'block universe' as a whole, in which all of time and the events of time are supposed to already be locked in place – past, present, *and future*. It just seems like physics wants it both ways. Actual causality and the illusion of causality. I mean, really...." His eyes rolled.

"You think so?" she asked, but not really in the interrogative. He was getting her undivided attention.

"Yeah...," he said, drawing out the word. "Physics wants to say time is only *sort of* real, which seems confusing – in a bad way, if you'll allow. And in both cases, whether in the causal or in the acausal, it seems to me that physicists think themselves as *observers*, outside the universe, in the audience, *peering in*, instead of as actors on the stage within the very complex play they're observing!"

He stopped, not wanting to overload the patience of his professor with perhaps unrelated questions that he wasn't sure made total sense. He was in high hopes that Professor Laplace would be a ready source of clear thinking for him. A sounding board. Someone who could help him sort out all the issues that had been roaming around in his head for so long.

All the while that Greyson had spoken his thoughts aloud, his eyes had looked everywhere but only rarely on her. He mostly looked at the floor, at the ceiling, and out the window, seeming to focus on infinity. Ariana picked up on this immediately. *The wheels are turning in his head again*, she thought to herself.

"Two things," said Ariana, stepping in when he paused.

"First, whether you realize it or not, you're not like other students. I can see that even from the lecture podium. You think *critically*. I can see the wheels turning in your head. That's quite remarkable, again whether or not you can see that for yourself just now. And, you're not just going down one line of thought. You're doing what the science of complexity is all about: being as critically inclusive as you can, from as many vantage points as you can. Physics' acceptance of causality here, nonacceptance there. And what is the meaning of *observer*? And the *observed*? How do

30

these, how *can* these all interrelate consistently, logically? Or are consistency and logic impossible? Greyson, you're headed in the right directions.

"Secondly, if you have a moment, I'd like to ask you to walk down the hall to meet someone. He's my advisor, Professor Porter. You know, Hans Porter, who won the Nobel a few years back?"

"Know? Of course I know *about* him, professor," Greyson said. "I'd be *thrilled* to meet him. Do you think he'd have time to meet *me*?"

"I'm sure of it," she said, encouraging him. "He'd be glad to make your acquaintance." Ariana stood up and together they exited her office and started down the hall. "We can continue our discussion in the near future," she said as they walked.

Thirty seconds later Ariana was knocking on Hans Porter's office door, with Greyson Landon standing to her side and a bit behind her. The Nobel laureate often stayed late, even on Friday afternoons.

"Come," said a voice from inside. When Ariana opened the door Hans looked up from his desk and said, "Oh, Ariana. My goodness, you've brought a guest. Who's the young gentleman with you?"

"Professor Porter, I'd like you to meet Greyson Landon, one of my freshman students. He dropped by my office, asking questions about my lecture, and I thought you might want to meet him."

Greyson thought, *Meet me? Why in the world would he want to meet me?* At only eighteen, with few people who could discuss his interests with him, he hadn't realized how much potential his questions had indicated.

"Of course," said Hans, rising from behind desk and reaching out to shake hands. "Greyson Landon is it? I'm Hans Porter. Call me Hans. As a matter of fact, if memory serves, I think Ariana mentioned you to me a while back. Delighted to meet you."

"Professor Porter, er…uh, Hans, I…." were all the words he could manage at that moment. He shook the hand of Nobel laureate with his eyes lowered. And then other words stumbled out as he raised his eyes to meet Professor Porter's: "I…I want say what an honor it is to meet you. I've read a lot of your work."

"Not at all, Greyson. Read my work, have you? Pleasure's mine. Good to meet you. Stop by the office anytime." Greyson couldn't believe his ears. Ariana smiled, looking at them both, and Greyson bowed a little toward the Nobel prize winner. Then the doctoral student and the freshman turned and withdrew from Hans Porter's office, closing the door behind them. Hans sat back down and resumed his work, grinning.

Little did Greyson realize that Hans and Ariana already had made a secret agreement. If she ever found a *live one*, he wanted to meet that student.

Chapter Six

Coincidence of Opposites

THE UNDULATING, RADIATING PULSE in the core room of the LDS continued to grow in size until the pulse *in* the core room became the pulse *of* the core room. Audibly, visually, palpably, viscerally the temporal phenomenon pulsed. Ariana, Greyson, Eloise, and Juan were all caught up inside of it now, inside of temporality, perhaps inside of time itself, and began to feel a marked depersonalizing effect. Staying conscious – conscious and *intact* – was a real struggle. Time was overtaking the space around them.

Then without warning, the rest of the hundreds of indicators on the monitors lit up again, signaling that all metrics were once more being gathered by the sensors and detectors and being saved on the LDS computers: metrics as in chronometrics, among other innumerable data – both from within the core itself and extending to the volume of the room.

One of the graphical indicators on a monitor displayed the strength of the manufactured gravitational field within the IGC during the incident. Ariana, the relativist, noticed that the reading right before shutdown of the orbitals indicated 1.2×10^{12} m/s^2, or a bit over one-half the gravity on the surface of a typical neutron star.[20] Since this was only one-half the machine's potential field strength, she guessed the weaker-than-expected gravity was the reason that the uncalibrated stabilizer did not precipitate the formation of a microscopic black hole.

---

[20] The time-dilation effect, which dramatically slowed the rate of decay or change of massive particles within the IGC's strong gravitational field, was also shown on screen, but the specifics of its effect on the evolving accident were undecipherable at this time. (Time dilation noticeably occurs as result of the velocity of a massive object moving at a significant fraction of the speed of light relative to a more stationary massive object, or as a result of a phenomenon being in a high gravitational field relative to being in a weaker gravitational field. Time dilation was one of components of time and of its arrow that was still thought by most relativists to be *sort of* real. At least the illusion itself was thought to be real – real enough, anyway.)

The indicators displaying the quantum information of the particles under the strong spacetime curvature clearly showed the accidental success: *Co-location of trillions of electrons and positrons has been achieved.* Greyson, on also seeing the verified co-location, felt a surge of excitement in addition to the fear of being in the core room just then. *The co-locational analytics were the first actual empirical evidence of what in recent hypotheses had been called a manufactured classical superposition.* Trillions of the two kinds of quantum particle had been physically forced together by the intense gravity into one *cohered* amalgam that comprised the quantum states of each kind. The modeling over the last few months had shown that the manufacture of a macroscopic superposition *could* possibly result from co-location, but no one knew whether it actually would be created or exactly how it might behave.

A temporal corollary of the Pauli exclusion principle, therefore, at least under these circumstances, did not occur. The temporal corollary of the Pauli exclusion principle seemed to be that there *was* no temporal corollary. Electrons and positrons *could* share, in other words, their respective quantum states, at least their time-flow states. In fact, it was now evident that those time states could become *fused*, or perhaps *entangled* was a better description. It appeared that what some early models had at first labeled bitemporal degeneracy pressure *was* the now-observed classical temporal superposition.

The *propagation* of the temporal superposition outside the actual inner core, the IGC, however, had *not* been predicted or modeled. And just as inexplicably, the anomaly still did not seem to be expanding beyond the room.

In short, an unprecedented large-scale total coherence of discrete particular opposites had occurred. Decohered particles had been cohered, fused, perhaps entangled into superposition. It was a first. *Quantum mechanics had been writ large and reversed.*[21] And since trillions of electrons

---

[21] In virtually all interpretations of quantum mechanics, even in the late twenty-first century, a state of superposition in undisturbed particles or complex waves was known to exist *until* observation, measurement, spontaneous reduction, or significant interaction with other parts of the system. The wave function of the superposition was said to *collapse*, in a probabilistic manner, *upon* observation, measurement, spontaneous reduction, or significant interaction. Opinion was divided regarding the precise cause or causes of collapse. Superposition, with multiple quantum states existing simultaneously, became *particularized* upon collapse into a particle with definite states. In this case, in the core

moving forward in time and trillions of positrons moving backward in time were involved, the classical superposition consisted of temporality in both directions at once, displacing space. *Purified time.* Perhaps entangled time. Normal time and anti-time were now in a sort of blurred synchronized fusion or entanglement within the walls of the core room. Formal analysis of the data was needed to further clarify the precise nature of the 'success.'

* * * * * * * * * * * *

Ariana tried to make additional sense of the undulating computer monitors as her pulsing mind reeled, caught within the radiating waves of temporal coherence.

"According to the data on-screen now, I *think*, we *are* inside some kind of growing temporal anomaly, as Grey thought," she said to the others with apprehension and a tinge of excitement as well. "We're *inside* the hole. The hole in time. Or the bubble *of* time. It's hard to say which, but the time metrics on the monitors appear to be, I don't know, *overlapping.* Like a vortex that's not really swirling, or a strange loop going back and forth. Time is somehow going in both directions at once, or that's how I'm reading it, anyway. I really don't know how to interpret it for sure. Temporal superposition isn't something we've seen before. Not to mention been inside of." She blinked a few times to help her stay focused. Everything was oscillating, *physically.*

She noticed that her colleagues appeared to nod in agreement before she had finished her initial phrase *According to the data.* She couldn't tell whether or not they had heard her finish her sentence before signaling their agreement. The moment was filled with countless unknowns. The monitors were now ablaze with continuously changing data, all of which were being recorded: data – empirical, real-time data, whatever *real-time* meant during this event. Whatever was happening, the constant state of change in the core room was being observed by the sensors and measured by the detectors, and already the quantum supercomputers on Level 16, nine hundred feet above them and three hundred feet below ground, had

---

room, the process *had been reversed*: Particular particles had been cohered into a superposition – of classical proportions.

begun to analyze the metrics generated by the phenomenon. The four of them were not, however, concentrating on data-capture at that particular moment. They were at ground-zero of a phenomenal reality that seemed as other-worldly as it was threatening.

As they all stood frozen in place, not knowing if it was safe to move or what to do, suddenly the pulsing noise increased in frequency and became lower in amplitude, and the physical, or at least visible, oscillations of the room also quickened and became less punctuated. The strong and slow pulsing wave that was manipulating the room became more of a vibration, weaker and quicker. Perhaps the anomaly was stabilizing.

Juan spoke next: "I'm not sure, but I think the temporal propagation may be dissipating. Maybe it's reached an equilibrium. Maybe it's a temporary thing and it's starting to collapse. I don't know. It seems sort of like the IGC gravitational field when we shut down the orbitals. I don't know if anything's going *away*, but…." He lost focus and stopped.

Eloise noticed in her haze that she seemed to know what he was going to say before he said it. She didn't know how. Greyson and Ariana also experienced this prescience, if you could call it that, and they all began to notice something else: It was as though their brains had *caught fire*, lighting up as suddenly as the monitors did a few moments ago – or was it hours? A lifetime ago? None of them could tell. Images the from past and present flashed through their minds in kaleidoscopic fashion, infinitely recursive, like mental fractals. Time surely *had* overtaken space. Thoughts came and went without words. Emotions piled up on each other without time to feel them. Their discrete memories all coincided, but with a nested quality to them, like the Russian dolls. Inside the temporal superposition, there wasn't one innate direction to time, and maybe not even two – perhaps many. They didn't know.

"I think it…I mean it looks like…," Juan started to say, but then he abruptly stopped. He was going to offer more about what he thought was going on in the core room, but gave up. He quickly realized that saying anything more in the middle of this unprecedented temporal maelstrom was wholly inadequate. He didn't *know* what was happening in the room or to them. For one thing, everything was happening too quickly. *Words were too slow, too linear, too blunt* – especially in the face of the unknown, and the unknown was upon them and currently out of analytical reach. It was enough just trying to stay conscious.

The four of them no longer felt like observers of a phenomenon, but the observed. Or at least the *observable*. They were inside a superposition, the first of its kind, and whatever was happening, it was certainly real, and it was certainly happening *now*. Their brains spun out of control, lost in a horizonless maze of unobstructed and interrelated imagery, thoughts, sounds, emotions – stretching from the room to infinity and back, it seemed. Then, just as their consciousness left them, the superposition vanished, and room suddenly went dark and silent.

Chapter Seven
Vital Signs

ARIANA LAPLACE AWOKE TWO DAYS LATER at 9:26 a.m., in Cambridge Medical Center to the sound of Beethoven's Grosse Fuge – that immensely interwoven double fugue, considered by many critics to be incomprehensible noise and by others to be the Holy Grail of string quartets. It was playing softly in the background. Greyson, having been released from the hospital earlier that morning, had told the medical staff how much Ariana enjoyed the piece, and he wanted to provide something familiar for her to listen to, since he had been told by the doctors that her neurological scans the day before indicated that she was responsive to auditory stimulus even though she was unconscious. He thought the music might seep in and provide some comfort.

Greyson was sitting at her bedside. Ariana's vital signs on the holographic biomonitor at the head of her bed were silently indicating normal, and her hypospray hydration regimen had been completed. The morning sun was peeking through the blinds of the room-length windows behind him. When Ariana stirred under the covers and opened her eyes a bit, she had to squint into the bright room.

"Where am I?" Ariana said through her clear plastic O2 mask when she saw Greyson next to her bed.

"Alice, you're awake!" he said smiling, donning his Bob hat to let her know she was alright. "Welcome back. You're in Cambridge Medical Center, still getting checked out. Don't worry, you're fine, they said. Vitals and neurological scans are normal." He leaned over and gently removed her O2 mask. "They said when you awoke I could remove the O2. Just a formality," he said, gesturing with the mask in his hand. Then he handed Ariana her glasses from the bedside table. "You're probably going to be released this afternoon or tomorrow, the doctors said. You're fine," he repeated.

"What about Eloise and Juan?" she said. "Are they okay? Where are they?"

"They're just down the hall," replied Greyson, pointing with the mask still in his hand toward the door of Ariana's private hospital room. "They're doing fine, too. Probably going home tomorrow."

Ariana put on her glasses and looked around the room. She used one hand to shield her eyes from the morning sun. Then she put both her hands out in front of her and looked at them before returning her gaze to her friend and colleague.

"What day is it, Grey?" she asked.

"It's the morning of May 20, 2079," said Greyson. "You've been out for a couple of days. I came to last night and they let me go earlier this morning. It's not quite three days since I phoned you at home in a panic from the LDS facility." And then he added, "Oh, and by the way, your department head is waiting for those grades – the three oral finals you gave just before I called." His familiar sheepish grin appeared and she managed to roll her eyes a bit.

Ariana slowly oriented herself as the memories of the accident in the LDS core room returned. Some of the fear also returned as she momentarily relived being inside the temporal superposition. Then the sound of a bladerunner taking off from the parking lot outside her window distracted her, bringing her back to the present moment. She glanced through the blinds toward the sound of the thrusters, and then looked back at Greyson.

"First of all, thanks for the Grosse Fuge," she said. "I'm assuming you're the culprit." He grinned. Then, more seriously, she said, "Grey, what in the hell happened? We were inside the temporal anomaly, I remember, and it was getting harder and harder to focus. The monitors were going crazy, I remember. And the pulsing, the vibration.... In the room *and* in my head.... The whole room was distorted and rippling, and I was getting really dizzy and confused. I must have blacked out."

"We all blacked out – just as everything finally shut down," he said. "The neurologists are still looking at our scans, but I think the neural pathways in our brains were temporarily overloaded inside the superposition. I'm sure we experienced sensory overload from both without and from within. We were inside of it and *it* was probably inside of us, too. That may not be the way the neurologists will put it, but I suspect that's what they'll mean."

"I can imagine," said Ariana. "Everything was happening so fast — inside my head, anyway. My brain felt like it was on fire…. Memories, thoughts, feelings, images…all overlapping. They all seemed…*mutually inclusive,* if you know what I mean. *Touching* each other, at *every* point. Like a dream. That's the way it felt, anyway. I know I might not be making much sense right now."

"No, no — me too. I felt the same way," said Greyson. "I think we all did. The co-location of the electrons and positrons caused a radiation of cohered time from the IGC into the core room. Or so it seems. We knew a classical superposition was a possibility, but we weren't prepared for the propagation. It stopped at the core room walls, thankfully. One of the things we have to figure out is why."

"We?" said Ariana, trying to read her friend. She was still a bit groggy.

Greyson paused and said flatly, "Yes, *we.* Beginning in a couple of weeks or so, if you're up to it. The LDS project team has asked us — you and me — to head up the investigation team. Not to look into the cause — we know the cause: the power surge. The investigation team will be tasked with interpreting all the data. What actually happened. And what it means. You and I are leading the team because, after all, we sort of have an advantage. We were there. We were *part* of it." And then he repeated, "*If* you're up to it."

"If I'm *up* to it?" Ariana exclaimed. "Grey, you know good and well I've been waiting my whole professional life for something like this! I'm a relativist who has a huge problem with relativity. That is, the *time* part. Time as illusion. Past, present, and future as illusion. My dissertation made an opposing argument, but in the end only *strongly suggested* the reality of time. But now we've just been inside a *temporal superposition.* I'm just hoping we can find something in the data that unequivocally confirms one way or the other whether or not *it was real.*"

Greyson smiled again and said, "I'm a quantum theorist, and I've got the same huge problem — you know that. And I do have a feeling that the data are going to tell us something…*new.* We've been where no one's been before, as the saying goes. So have the sensors and detectors in the core room. The scans may have even caught some of our brain activity in the process – we were, after all, in the crosshairs."

"Who's on the team?" Ariana inquired, jumping ahead.

"Physicists, neurologists, molecular biologists, and quantum biochemists, I'm sure," he replied. "Probably others, too. MIT and the Institute have just started recruiting. Eloise and Juan of course. Between all of us, I think the science of complexity is about to show us a whole new gear."[22]

Then his tone became uncharacteristically serious as he carefully measured his words: "A classical superposition, Professor Laplace, and a classical *temporal* superposition – that's a *big* first. For everybody." And then, almost whispering, he looked her straight in the eye and repeated the obvious: "And we were there, Ariana. We were *there*. We were *inside* the thing."

She slowly nodded without speaking. She was thinking of her late mentor, Hans Porter, and how she wished he could have been a part of all this. For Hans, nothing was more thrilling than being on the brink of discovery. Then her eyes started darting, not coming to rest on anything in particular. Her mind had begun to scan the possibilities of what the future might have in store. Greyson recognized the pattern, and silently leaned back in admiration. He was reminded him of his undergraduate days at Caltech, with Ariana lecturing at the podium. Once again, he could see the wheels turning in *her* head.

---

[22] The reader will remember that the late twenty-first-century emerging science of complexity concerned an open acknowledgement that everything influences everything else – in a interdependent and often nonlinear or dynamical way. The science of complexity resists 1) the study of *idealized* phenomena consisting of an artificially isolated subsystem of a larger system for purpose of convenience, and relatedly, 2) parochially excluding extradisciplinary scientific findings that could affect the conclusions of one's own intradisciplinary research. In physics, both of these narrow viewpoints were colloquially called doing 'physics in a box.'

Chapter Eight

The Investigation

THE LDS ACCIDENT INVESTIGATION TEAM consisted of sixty-seven international scientists from multiple physical disciplines (including twelve Nobel prize winners), and began the work of combing through the data exactly two weeks later, with an initial plenary session on June 3, 2079 at MIT. (The seasonal timing of the accident was a fortunate happenstance due to the summer academic recess.) Some of the scientists set up temporary residence at MIT for the project, while others worked remotely in their own university labs and commuted periodically for plenary sessions. All sixty-seven were present for the June 3 meeting.

Three main types of data had been gathered in the core room during the incident: 1) gravitational field, 2) wave/particle and quantum interaction, and 3) chronometric. Gravitational field sensors had measured the warping of spacetime inside the Inner Gravitational Chamber. Quantum detectors were designed to identify all known matter and energy/force particles in the Standard Model, plus exotic particles, and they were also configured to detect all particle interactions possible during the co-location, given the energy level of the equipment involved. Chronometric probes were in place to gauge the electron vibrations of strategically placed caesium atoms and, for extremely precise cross-reference, the quark vibrations in the atoms' respective nucleons.

The team of sixty-seven scientists was divided into three groups by the same categories – gravitational field, quantum, and chronometric – with Ariana and Greyson floating between groups as necessary and coordinating the data analysis. Sub-groups of specific specialty fields were also formed, all communicating freely with each other thanks to the now-accepted paradigm of complexity. As Greyson had indicated to Ariana, not only physicists, but biochemists, molecular biologists, neuroscientists, and related physical scientists participated in the analysis.

Gravity, quantum mechanics, and time were all, of course, familiar aspects of theoretical and experimental physics. What was new was the very large temporal superposition, and most importantly the new perspective this phenomenon had potentially given the world. *For the first time, a macroscopic superposition had been created from discrete quantum particles, temporal in nature, marking time in opposite directions, and this meant that the team would have the first-ever opportunity to, in some new way, hopefully, examine time from the outside looking in.* Their vantage point would not be absolutely outside of time, of course, since they themselves obviously still participated *in* time, but they would be closer than anyone had ever been to an external temporal perspective.

* * * * * * * * * * * *

The June 3 meeting began at 9:00 a.m. in Frank Wilczek Hall at MIT, with Ariana at the podium. The hall featured stadium seating and was filled to capacity. The excitement in the room that morning was palpable – the scientists were actively and freely conversing, some rather loudly, with each other before the start of the meeting. The sound of laughter often punctuated the steady buzz of the casual, pre-meeting colloquies. An overflow crowd, which included several thousand scientists from around the world, also attended the meeting on livestream.

"Ladies and gentlemen, welcome," said Ariana to the team at 9:00 a.m. sharp, her pleasant voice amplified and broadcast by the holographic LRT microphone floating in front of her.[23] The conversation in the room subsided quickly. "I'm Ariana Laplace, relativity and quantum dynamics at the Institute for Advanced Study at Princeton. I'll be assisted in the coordination of the LDS investigation by Greyson Landon, quantum mechanics, also at the Institute. You've all received your project packets, and you know your groups, sub-groups, lab locations, and assignments."

And then she went to the heart of the matter: "We have before us an extraordinary opportunity in the study of the incident at the LDS: It was, as you know, an accidental *success*. For the first time, particulate matter was, under strong gravity, fused or entangled into a superposition,

---

[23] LRT stands for laser radio transmitter, which converts low-frequency laser light into radio waves for purpose of communication. LRT communication had been in wide commercial use since the 2050s.

temporal in nature and classical in size. Time-forward electrons and time-reverse positrons were cohered, producing a temporal superposition that propagated from the Inner Gravitational Chamber to the volume of the LDS core room. The data from the incident have been gathered for your analysis. One of our main goals is to use our unprecedented external*istic* vantage point on the temporal anomaly to, if possible, make progress on empirically deciding what time *really* is all about. That is, whether or not there is a real, physical nature to time – if the past *was* real, if the present *is* real, and if the future is open to any number of possibilities that *will be* real. In other words, in contradistinction to the relativistic block universe theory, we will attempt to ascertain if there is, in fact, something intrinsically and fundamentally *real* about the flow of time. And if so – *if so* – do we, then, in point of fact, have *agency, opening up* the future for our active and dynamic *participation?* Ladies and gentlemen, these are big questions, *very* big questions, as you well know. Perhaps this is the moment in history when, thanks to your analysis, the answers will be unveiled."

She went on the explain some of the particulars of how the accident started and evolved. Other members of the team's leadership then provided further overview and research parameters. Ariana and Greyson concluded the plenary session by fielding questions. At 12:00 p.m., the session ended and the team was dismissed to their respective research areas and assignments. The work began apace that afternoon, and expectations were high.

* * * * * * * * * * * * *

It took only three weeks for the discovery process to yield the first results. On June 24, Greyson's daily 3:00 p.m. collaboration visit to Ariana's project office at MIT began a bit earlier than usual. That day, he unexpectedly appeared in her office doorway at 1:42 p.m.

"Grey, you're a bit early today. Good news?" she asked, looking up from the screenpad portable computer on her desk.

"Well, professor," he said formally, "I have some rather perturbing information for you." He then broke into a wide-eyed smile. "It appears we now know why the superposition stopped at the core walls and then disappeared just as the room went dark. One of Juan's guesses during the event was right."

"It collapsed under the observation of the sensors and detectors," she said, looking at him. "Right?"[24]

"Yes," he said, nodding, not at all surprised by her insightful response. "And maybe also because of *our* observation, inside, but we don't know that part for sure. The neurophysicists and psychobiologists haven't finally weighed in yet. *But...*that's not all...." he added, and then paused.

It was a pregnant pause, a very purposeful pause. Before he spoke again, he wanted to do Ariana the deferential courtesy of allowing her to prompt him. The study of time, after all, had been her most important focus since her doctoral days under Hans Porter. She undoubtedly knew the direction his early briefing was headed just from the look on his face. Ariana took the hint, and not so absent-mindedly took off her glasses and squeezed the bridge of her nose. She wanted to clear her mind to better take in his next words, which just might signal one of the most important scientific discoveries in history. She released her nose, put her glasses back on, and looked at Greyson again.

"Tell me about the chronometrics," she said.

---

[24] In quantum mechanics, according to some interpretations, a particle (or complex wave) is in superposition – i.e. in a number of quantum states at once – until observed or measured by a detector of some kind. Upon observation or measurement, the particle's superposition collapses by a process known as decoherence, governed by Schrödinger's probabilistic equation of the wavefunction, into a discrete particle with a known quantum state (such as spin or location). Other interpretations vary with regard to this collapse or "reduction." For instance, as mentioned above, significant interaction with another particle in the same system also is widely thought to cause the superposition to be "disturbed" and thus collapse. Another interpretation posits that superposition collapses spontaneously, causing a cascade of collapse, creating the discrete macroscopic objects of the everyday world. Other interpretations are also current, and were, in fact, still in play during the late twenty-first century.

Chapter Nine

The Temple of Time

"THE CHRONOMETRICS," SAID GREYSON, not missing a beat and measuring his words carefully, "have – just within the last couple of hours – preliminarily indicated what may turn out to be both a stitch *and* a hitch in time."

"You mean we may have found something *physical* in the classical superposition of time – physical both a *continuous* temporal *quality* and a *discrete* temporal *quantity*," she said, rapidly translating his terms of art into something more conducive to further rational discussion. Her wheels were turning so fast that she was barely conscious of the intense rush of excitement she was feeling.

"We *think* so," said Greyson. "The normal caesium electron vibrations picked up what the monitors were displaying that night as basically unintelligible nonsense – the strange vortex or looping of time inside the superposition. Time being in a sort of a *chaotic suspension* due to the co-location of the time-forward electrons and the time-reverse positrons. A temporal suspension independent from *space* – as least to some degree. But what the software wasn't designed to display on the monitors was the infinitesimal hitch in the quark vibrations. The much faster *quark* vibrations in the caesium nucleons *seem* to be periodically *interrupted* by what may just turn out to be tiny *punctuations* in time – at or near the Planck scale.[25] We're not sure yet. But there may be *particles*, Ariana – *bits of time* interacting with everything else at the most fundamental level of physical reality. Sort of like the Higgs."

He stopped there. That was basically all the information he had at the moment, and he had come over early for their daily meeting only for a

---

[25] The Planck scale, named for theoretical physicist Max Planck (1858-1947), describes various units of the physical world – such as length, time, mass, energy, and temperature – at the smallest or lowest of scales, below which classical physics ceases to make sense and quantum mechanics assumes dominance.

cursory briefing. In this case, cursory was *plenty*. Besides, he wanted Ariana's spontaneous input on the potentially historic news he had just unloaded on his former physics professor.

"So," she continued for him, looking off into the distance, "quanta of time. If that's the case, that means that there may be a temporal *field* as well, where the evanescent excitations of time manifest themselves – the bits or quantized particles. Or maybe the particles are actually waves until observation or measurement, like everything else – whatever that might mean in the case of time. And then there's the question of the past, present, and future." Then softly, almost poetically, she said slowly, as if dictating or lecturing: *"How might these initial temporal indications address the tenses of existence?"* After a moment of reflection on that statement, she raised her voice and stated confidently, "We're getting close, Grey – I can smell it! I think it's time we paid our next official visit to the chronometrics lab."

"They're already expecting us," he said.

Ariana turned off her computer and picked up her screenpad to take along for recording and notation. They left her office and quickly walked the quarter mile across the MIT campus to the chronometrics lab. On the way, they risked jumping the gun by experimenting with nomenclature to see how the terms rolled off the tongue and sounded to the ear. Before they reached the lab building, they had already made up their minds. If in fact there *were* particles of time, they should be called *chronons*.

* * * * * * * * * * * *

The chronometrics group leader was Professor Antonio Ghirardi, the famous temporal physicist from Trieste, and he was waiting for them at the lab. He had been involved with the LDS project since its inception, and was one of the most respected members of the investigation team. At sixty-five, with a shiny horseshoe-bald head, grey-white sidewalls, and dark-rimmed circular glasses, he was the picture of the old-school professor, and he had been on the front lines of temporal theory for forty years.

Professor Ghirardi was beaming when the two arrived, and was the first to speak, his old-fashioned European demeanor on full display.

"Professor Laplace," he said with his heavy Italian accent, more than slightly bowing toward her, "a pleasure to see you, especially under such auspicious circumstances." His English was perfect. With a twinkle in his eye, he glanced over at Greyson for just a moment since the two of them had already spent most of the morning together, scrutinizing the data. Then his eyes turned back to Ariana as he straightened from his bow. She and Professor Ghirardi had met years earlier at a conference at Stanford, and had spoken briefly several times during the LDS analysis, but they didn't know each other well.

"*Ariana*, if you please," she said smiling, cordially asserting her American penchant for personal relationship over titular observance. "We've been formal far too long."

"Ariana it is," said Professor Ghirardi. "And I would be grateful if you called me Antonio."

Formalities and informalities out of the way, Ariana cut right to the chase: "Tell me what you've got, Antonio," she said. "*Auspicious*, you say. What are we looking at?"

"Well, to tell you the truth, we're not a hundred percent sure *what* we're seeing. But there's *something* there. I'd like you personally to take a close look at the data — the quark data in particular, but the general caesium electron vibrations as well. I say *personally* because, if you'll allow me to say, some years ago I read your dissertation and was very impressed. Your advisor Hans Porter, in fact, was the one who recommended it to me, and so of course I took a look. Your rather heterodox theories looked very sound indeed. I had never thought about time that way. And the hypothetical parts of your research also seemed to me to be quite, shall we say, refreshing — novel, in a *compelling* way. It seemed to me that despite your departure from convention you made a very intriguing case.

"And in point of fact, Ariana, I believe we may be looking at data right here and now that support the preliminary conclusions you reached in your work under my old friend Hans. We have the technology now, thanks to people like Dr. Bardier and Dr. Marcelino here at MIT. An initial experiment on the nature of time has been completed, accidental component notwithstanding. A classically sized temporal superposition was created, allowing us the chance to really get a look at time from a somewhat external viewpoint. And now, the data are in hand."

"Data in support of my hypothesis," she said, mostly to herself. And then to Antonio and Greyson, "Well, that *would* be something, wouldn't it? Show me the numbers."

* * * * * * * * * * * * *

Ariana, Greyson, and Professor Ghirardi spent the next several weeks studying the data together. The caesium atoms, whose electrons normally vibrated at over nine billion times per second when exposed to certain wavelengths of light,[26] had acted a bit strangely during the incident. Ariana parsed the numbers and after several days concluded that a certain turbulent chaos had been introduced into the electrons' otherwise steady and continuous stream of energy vibrations. The nature of the chaos had an unpredictable pattern in it, she determined, a hidden order, similar to the unpredictable order tucked away in all the other ubiquitous chaos of nature.[27] In addition to the chaos in the frequency of the electron vibrations, the *amplitude* or energy level of the vibrations was inexplicably high, as though the caesium had been dipped into something that was possessed of an intrinsic *vitality*. Alternatively, it could have been that the atoms had been freed from a burden or a weight or a friction of some kind while in the temporal superposition. The extra energy had been just enough to trigger the chaotic pattern. Years ago, in her dissertation, Ariana had hypothesized the occurrence of such a sustained

---

[26] The precise frequency is 9,192,631,770 cycles per second, or hertz (abbreviated Hz). This is the rate of change in the energy state of the electrons of caesium-133 atoms when exposed to electromagnetic radiation (i.e. light) in the microwave range of the radio wave spectrum.

[27] In general, chaos is defined as a type of nonlinear, dynamical behavior in a system where there exists an extremely sensitive dependence on initial conditions. In other words, chaos occurs when a small change in input conditions results in a disproportionately large – and *unpredictable* – change in system output. Chaos has been observed in the innumerable phenomena of nature, from climate systems to coastlines to leaky faucets to globular star clusters to the distribution of galaxies in the universe at large. Chaos, in other words, appears to be 'baked in the cake' of nature.

The science of chaos had helped fuel the rise of *the science of complexity*, the new paradigm of the late twenty-first century, where everything was seen to influence everything else.

For further reference, cf. *Chaos: Making a New Science* by James Gleick (Penguin Books, 1987, 2008), and the more recent *Chaos and Complexity: The Science of Interrelationships* by Ricardo Flores Figueroa (Oxford University Press, 2058).

energy boost might initiate chaos, though she had to get creative in the mathematics when infinities arose.

With regard to the caesium *quark* data, however, something more *punctuated* presented itself, as Greyson had noted to her earlier. The quarks in the nuclear protons and neutrons, too, seemed to have been given a *kick* of some sort as the superposition filled the room, though not in the relatively continuous way of the atoms' electron vibrations. Using the lab's quantum computer for purpose of speed and precision, she determined that every so often – every 10^{-24} seconds, to be exact[28] – the quarks shook or jumped *more than usual* by exactly the same discrete amount. The kick was too small and too frequent to be observed in the noise of the electron vibrations, but it was clearly present in the behavior of the quarks.

"What do you make of that, Ariana?" said Professor Ghirardi, two weeks into the analysis, after the numbers became clear. "The energy spikes – the extra, what shall we call it, *buoyancy* in the electron and quark vibrations? It's manifesting differently in each case."

"I calculated these possibilities in my dissertation research, as you may recall," said Ariana. "I didn't make the association then, but I think the closest analogy we may have is what Grey noted earlier in my office – it's like the Higgs field. As matter gains its mass due to its interaction with the Higgs boson in Higgs field, it looks like *time* gains a kind of stability or rate plus a *direction* due to its interaction with the three large dimensions of space. I believe the energy spike in both the caesium electrons and quarks represents time *freed from the drag of space*. Or freed from *some* of the drag of space, anyway. The large temporal superposition in the core room displaced much of the core room space. Not all the space, but much of it. And time got a kick in the pants."

And then she spoke words that were most especially memorable – not unlike other memorable words spoken by the giants, often extemporaneously, and then recorded for posterity in the annals of achievement. Ariana said: *"And I hardly think it's possible to kick an illusion in the pants. I think we're on the verge, gentlemen, of discovering nothing less than the fundamental physical reality of time."*

---

[28] 10^{-24} seconds is one septillionth of a second, also called a yoctosecond.

Greyson was listening intently to her pivotal words, of course, but all the while she was speaking, the only thing he *saw* were the wheels turning in her head -- wheels free from the drag that inhabits and inhibits all but the rarest of minds. He was in the presence of genius at work and at play, and he knew he was witnessing history unfold before him.

Chapter Ten

New Beginnings

MIT WAS THE CENTER OF THE SCIENTIFIC UNIVERSE during the summer of 2079. Rumors of discovery about time had traveled quickly in the academic community, though nothing official had yet been announced. Professor Ghirardi joined Ariana and Greyson in leading the LDS analysis, all of them working out of the chronometrics lab, which had become the hub of discovery. Collaborating with the rest of the sixty-seven member team, the three of them spent the rest of the summer parsing the data, reviewing the Level 16 quantum supercomputer analysis, painstakingly checking and double-checking their own calculations as well as those of others, and solidifying their conclusions. Despite the long hours of work involved, it was an exhilarating summer for them. They all agreed that there was no excitement in the world like having exclusive empirical evidence at your fingertips – *something nobody else in the world knows* – pointing toward a potential scientific breakthrough and a truly new paradigm for understanding the physical world.

Finally, on August 29, 2079 at 1:00 p.m. Eastern Daylight Time, the team convened in plenary for the last time for the purpose of announcing its findings. They met in the recently refurbished Kresge Auditorium, the largest hall at MIT, with seating for over twelve hundred. Scientists, teachers, philosophers, dignitaries, and press from all over the world were invited and in attendance. (The hall was full, needless to say, and the parking lots at MIT were filled with bladerunners equipped with long-range boosters.) The massive gathering was designed primarily to be the official pre-publication summary of the discoveries, but also served as a rather upscale press conference, complete with global livestream coverage.[29]

---

[29] The team's complete findings were already scheduled for an October publication in the prestigious *Physical Review Letters*, with Ariana Laplace, Antonio Ghirardi, and Greyson Landon as lead authors.

Gregor Meiringen, the MIT chancellor, himself a biophysicist by training, began the proceedings, and after a short address introduced Professor Ghirardi, who, as a temporal physicist and a senior member of the LDS team, presided over the assembly. As Professor Ghirardi was being introduced, he rose from his chair in the row of seats on the stage, occupied by leaders of the LDS team, and proceeded toward the podium and the chancellor.

"Thank you very much, Chancellor Meiringen," said Professor Ghirardi at the podium into the floating LRT microphone in front of him. Behind him, displayed on the built-in, stage-width macroscreen was a large image of the LDS core room with the following words overlaid in large typeface:

The Nature of Time
Presented by MIT and The Institute for Advanced Study
Tuesday, August 29, 2079, 1:00 p.m.

"Ladies and gentlemen," said Professor Ghirardi, "On behalf of MIT, the Institute, and the LDS team, I want to welcome all of you — colleagues, dignitaries, and the public from around the world — to this momentous event. I stand before you with extreme pleasure at what will no doubt be the culmination of my own career and, perhaps, that of many others here as well.

"For twenty-five hundred years, philosophers and scientists alike have grappled methodically with the nature of time. Albert Einstein, in his theories of relativity in the early twentieth century, provided the basis for our current, conventional wisdom. Time — that is, the distinction between past, present, and future — is but a stubbornly persistent illusion, he said in one way or another throughout his life. For the past one hundred fifty years, the evidence at hand pointed to the fundamental illusory nature of time's passage, confined as a true but static dimension of our four-dimensional universe.

"And yet for some, this deterministic pronouncement on the nature of reality has always been shaded by lingering questions. Doubt still remained, at least in the minds of some. Is time *in fact* an illusion, or is it possible that time is *real*, despite what relativity tells us? Is the universe absolutely constrained by a blocked-and-locked determinism, as we physicists sometimes put it, or is it still somehow open to possibility, surprise, and spontaneity – based on things like quantum uncertainty, on the small scale, and human agency, on the large? Despite the discoveries of Einstein, a tension has still lingered between our common sense experience of time and what may actually lie beneath that experience.

"Now, thanks to the work of people here at the Massachusetts Institute of Technology, the Institute for Advanced Study at Princeton University, and that of many, many hundreds of other scientists, engineers, and technicians around the world, we on the LDS team are prepared today to announce an answer to the stubborn and persistent *questions* regarding the nature of time: *And it's an answer that eclipses Einstein.*

"And with that said, I'd like to introduce you to my esteemed colleague, Professor Laplace, relativity and quantum dynamics at the Institute for Advanced Study. She was the lead researcher in our work this summer, and she'll take us forward from here this afternoon. Ladies and gentlemen, may I present Professor Ariana Laplace."

Ariana rose from her chair on the stage and walked to the podium to the sound of vigorous applause. The audience at Kresge knew she had been at the forefront of the discoveries, and that her presentation would be the main attraction of the afternoon. When she arrived at the podium, Professor Ghirardi shook her hand and again, this time in front of the world, bowed slightly before her.

"Thank you, Antonio," said Ariana quietly, returning his bow, and then she faced the audience. She couldn't help but smile a bit as the applause continued for a few more seconds.

"Thank you," she said to the gathering. "The complete findings of the LDS investigation team will be published soon, so today I'll just be going over the highlights. The main points of our overview will be displayed on the macroscreen behind me.

"As you may be aware, on May 17 of this year, while the Lepton Degeneracy Stabilizer, or LDS, was in its final testing phase, we experienced a power surge. An accident occurred. To say the least, it was a fortunate accident, leading to dramatic results.

"The experiment involved the co-location of electrons, which move forward in time, and positrons, which move backward in time. The experiment was undertaken in order to hopefully unveil new information on the fundamental nature *of* time. This co-location of particles was accomplished under an extremely strong, manufactured gravitational field, generated by the LDS.

"The accident, to repeat, was a success. As a result of the co-location of electrons and positrons, a classically sized superposition was created, *temporal* in nature. We created what might loosely be called a temporal hole in space or a bubble of *purified time*, as we have begun to call it. That is to say, the particulates of the forward and reverse arrows of time were fused into a macroscopic superposition comprising *both* directions at once.

"Due to the trillions of particles involved, with more flooding the inner-core compartment every second and undergoing co-location, the superposition grew in size from the initial target area – the inner chamber of the LDS – until it filled the entire core room. Prior to the test runs of the LDS, we had calculated that a temporal superposition was a possible outcome of the experiment, but its propagation was, frankly, a surprise. The superposition seemed to take on a life of its own due to the increasing number of particles being pumped into the inner chamber. Several of us were in the core room when propagation occurred. It was quite disorienting for us, and we all were admitted to hospital for a few days for tests and observations. Thankfully, we came through unscathed. The superposition finally and suddenly collapsed under the observation and measurement of the sensors and detectors. But it did *not* collapse until we had our data in hand.

"After weeks of evaluating the data measured in the core room, we have concluded the following: The manufactured classical temporal superposition was, in fact, time being separated from normal spacetime. Time was leveraged, if you will – leveraged *free from the drag of normal spacetime.* The image behind me now is a photograph from that moment, taken with a camera at the LDS just outside the core room and thus beyond the effects of the temporal superposition."

At seeing the photograph, the audience gasped. The gasp was followed by a collective under-the-breath sound of discussion in the crowd. The image of the *physically* undulating and thus distorted room was something they had never seen before – in an undoctored photograph, at any rate. Ariana continued:

"We found solid chronometric evidence of time supplanting space in both the caesium electron vibrations, or energy transitions, *and* in the quark vibrations as measured by the sensors.

"In the electron vibrations, during the propagation of the superposition into the room, we detected a continuous surge of energy. The caesium electron vibrations increased in frequency from over nine billion times per second to twelve billion times per second. In addition, the pattern of electron vibration, usually absolutely steady, acquired a chaotic or turbulent imprint, as so often happens in nature when you 'turn up the knob' on an energy source.

"Regarding the much faster quark vibrations, fascinatingly, we found that frequency remained the same, with one *very* significant exception: Every 10^{-24} seconds, to be exact – that is, every trillion trillionth of a second – the energy level of quark vibration spiked by 4.669%. Not much, but clearly a discrete kick, a quantized periodic *punctuation*. Ladies and gentlemen, we have found *particles* of time. At the smallest and fastest scales of reality, time has a *granularity* to it. Time is quantum in nature. We're calling the punctuations, the particles, the quanta of time *chronons.*"

Once again, the gasps from the audience were audible, and spontaneous *sotto voce* discussion broke out followed by the ascendant sound of applause that lasted for a good fifteen seconds.

"Time, in other words," Ariana continued, "is physical in nature. Time is fundamental. Time is real. And, we're still exploring the possibility – the *possibility* – that the quanta of time are entangled – *temporally entangled.* This would go a long way to understanding how discrete quanta can continuously *flow*. We expect to have more to say on this in publication.

"The bottom-line is: Time is not just a measure of change. Time itself is *part* of change. Time continually and yet discretely *refreshes* itself as a fundamental constituent of our spacetime reality. By analogy, just as virtual particles pop into existence from the very fabric of spacetime, filling it – spontaneously, randomly, constantly – so *chronons* appear with equal constancy, filling the fabric of *space*, in turn generating space*time*. The chronons comprise a constancy that in fact *enables* change. Every moment of time is, in fact, a new moment of time, filled with endless possibility, now and for the future.

"This quantum font of time, ladies and gentlemen, is precisely the reason the block universe theory is incomplete and, ultimately, wrong. The deterministic aspect of Einstein's relativity is ignorant of the chronon. Relativity has assumed that time is a permanent layer of reality, a fixity, when in fact time is not really a layer but an endless punctuation, an endless series of *opportunities* that renews itself at every moment *in* time and at every point in space. Determinism, in the throes of death these last one hundred years or so, has finally died. Its obituary may finally be written. The future is not just based on the causal past, *but on the present moment as well.* And we live in the present moment – always. Every one of our nows is a *new* now, and all the infinite complexities in reality, all the interdependent events in nature everywhere, all the actions and all the thoughts of all the conscious beings in all the universe have a sure and certain impact on this now, and so…on the future."

With that she concluded her address, and the audience members rose to their feet with an applause that signaled they knew they were in the presence of history being made in front of them. Ariana turned to the row of chairs behind her, first looking at Greyson, and with moist eyes and a hand gesture asked the LDS team representatives on the stage to rise in order to share the moment.

* * * * * * * * * * * * * *

The year was 2082, and the date was October 8. It had been a little over three years since the audience at the Kresge Auditorium at MIT had stood to give Ariana Laplace a three-minute ovation. The time was 3:30 in the morning, Eastern Daylight Time, in Princeton, New Jersey. The phone rang in Ariana's home. She awoke with a start, and instinctively, as always, said, "Answer, voice only." The holophone screen materialized in front of her. She just had time to put on her glasses when she realized she had forgotten to deactivate caller ID. Before the voice on the other end of the phone had a chance to speak, the screen displayed the identification of the caller. In the light-hearted vernacular that had become traditional for such annual phone calls, made typically to two or three physicists in the world every October, the message on the screen simply read: *The Swedish Prize Committee.*

Acknowledgments

This is my first attempt at a novel. After spending some six or seven years reading theoretical physics books, articles, and papers, as well as a few related works in other physical sciences, I felt the need to actually write about physics in a rather formal way but without the fear of getting something wrong. A novel seemed like a good idea. When writing about physics, especially without using mathematics (in which I am not trained), getting something wrong is very easy to do, especially for an amateur physicist. I know that much. In *theoretical* physics (as that adjective is generally used), especially, mentioning one point of view in one particular context always begs the articulation of that point of view in other contexts, and it also begs mention of entirely different points of view on the same general topic. While I am trained to cover all the usual bases in my primary field (religious studies), my knowledge of physics is grievously inadequate for a thoroughly accurate and exhaustive presentation, even assuming a narrow focus. This short novel seemed like a somewhat serious and yet very enjoyable way to experiment with writing passionately about the scientific concepts that have occupied so much of my thought in recent years.

Having said that, the reader should be aware that in this book I have taken a great number of purposeful liberties with physics, and I take some pride in knowing just *where* I have used creative license. That was part of the fun! But in general, in writing *Ad Infinitum* I tried to begin as close as I could to valid physical fact, or some current interpretation of physical phenomena, and then I proceeded impenitently to bend both convention and controversy in the direction of what I hope is a good story. The work is really a romance novel about time.

I had a target audience in mind. *Ad Infinitum* is intended for people with interest or background in physics, but it's also for science and science fiction enthusiasts in general. I have attempted to introduce and explain some of the 'technical' concepts (to the best of my ability) and historical personages as I go along, especially in the footnotes, but it may seem to some readers as though I have 'started in the middle.' Apologies if my treatment (and mistreatment) of the science gets in the way of the fiction.

A comprehensive list of all the theorists, experimentalists, educators, and authors who have influenced me in my recent scientific education would be unwieldy here; however, I must mention a few. Among the physicists themselves,

Richard P. Feynman, Kip Thorne, Giancarlo Ghirardi, John Archibald Wheeler, Stephen Hawking, and Lee Smolin have been heavily influential. In the world of cognitive neuroscience, Michael S. Gazzaniga (the father of the field) stands out. The most literarily talented and thorough science *writer* I have read is James Gleick. I have also been inspired by the philosophy of science writings of Tim Maudlin and Roberto Mangabeira Unger. Additional scientific inspiration has come from Brian Cox, Sean Carroll, Max Tegmark, Carlo Rovelli, and Brian Greene.

Otherwise, I am particularly indebted to Bob and Sachiko Morrell, who over the years have taught me that language is but a blunt instrument and sometimes an altogether counterproductive obstacle, and to my good friend Ricardo Flores, who, as full professor of physics here in St. Louis, gladly clarified much of what I found confusing in the literature.

For reading my manuscript and providing both encouragement and a number of instructive suggestions, I am indebted to Jorge Marzocchini, to my father, Harry Scott, and to his friend, Harry Brady.

Most especially, I am grateful to my editors-in-chief: my daughter, Sarah Scott, and her husband, Brett Stults. Sarah provided me with her flawless literary and stylistic guidance as well as a careful, penultimate proofing of the manuscript. Brett gladly measured my small work against the canon of science fiction literature, of which he has a very comprehensive and insightful knowledge, and gave me discerning and thoughtful suggestions.

Randall R. Scott
St. Louis, Missouri
August 24, 2020

Made in the USA
Las Vegas, NV
07 April 2021

Randy Scott is retired and lives in St. Louis, Missouri. An academic pedestrian of no great importance for many years, his current interests include theoretical physics; literature; neuroscience; orchestral composition; religious and psychological studies; Japanese literary and emotional aesthetics; complexity and approximation; and, most especially, watching his granddaughter grow up in California.

The year is 2079, and the very nature of time is under experimental investigation by leading scientific specialists in classical relativity *and* quantum mechanics from around the world.

Journey into the near future to explore, with the characters of this novel, the nature of time, free will, and the new paradigm of complexity. Is the flow of time -- past, present, and future -- an illusion, as Einstein's theories of relativity suggest? Is the unfolding of reality therefore already determined in what has been called the "block universe"? Or is the flow of time somehow fundamental, rendering the present moment real and the future open -- open to human agency, to possibility, to surprise? Perhaps only an accident in the lab will actually unveil what time is all about.

ISBN 9798679132276